15.95

THE GIRL ON THE YELLOW GIRAFFE

By Ronald Himler

Star Bright Books
New York

Published in the United States of America by Star Bright Books, Inc., New York.
The name Star Bright Books and the Star Bright Books logo are registered
trademarks of Star Bright Books, Inc. Please visit www.starbrightbooks.com.

ISBN 1-932065-93-8
Printed in China 9 8 7 6 5 4 3 2 1

Library of Congress Cataloging-in-Publication Data

Himler, Ronald.
  The girl on the yellow giraffe / by Ronald Himler.
      p. cm.
  Summary: While riding her toy giraffe from her apartment to a city park and back,
a girl's fantasies transport her to a land of giants, dragons, and magicians.
  ISBN 1-932065-93-8
  [1. City and town life--Fiction.] I. Title.
PZ7.H5684Gi 2004
[E]--dc22
                                      2004002160

For Anna, again.

— R.H.

There once was a girl on a yellow giraffe.
She lived in a beautiful stone castle.

Inside the castle there was a magic box.
It carried her gently down. . .

to the land of the giants.

She was not afraid.

She said hello to everyone.
And everyone said hello to her.

She visited strange places. . .

and saw many wonderful things.

She saw a wizard,

a magician in a blue hat,

and monsters and dragons.

Sometimes the road was rough.

Sometimes the road was smooth.

She played in a garden.

It had a fountain.

She watched games. . .

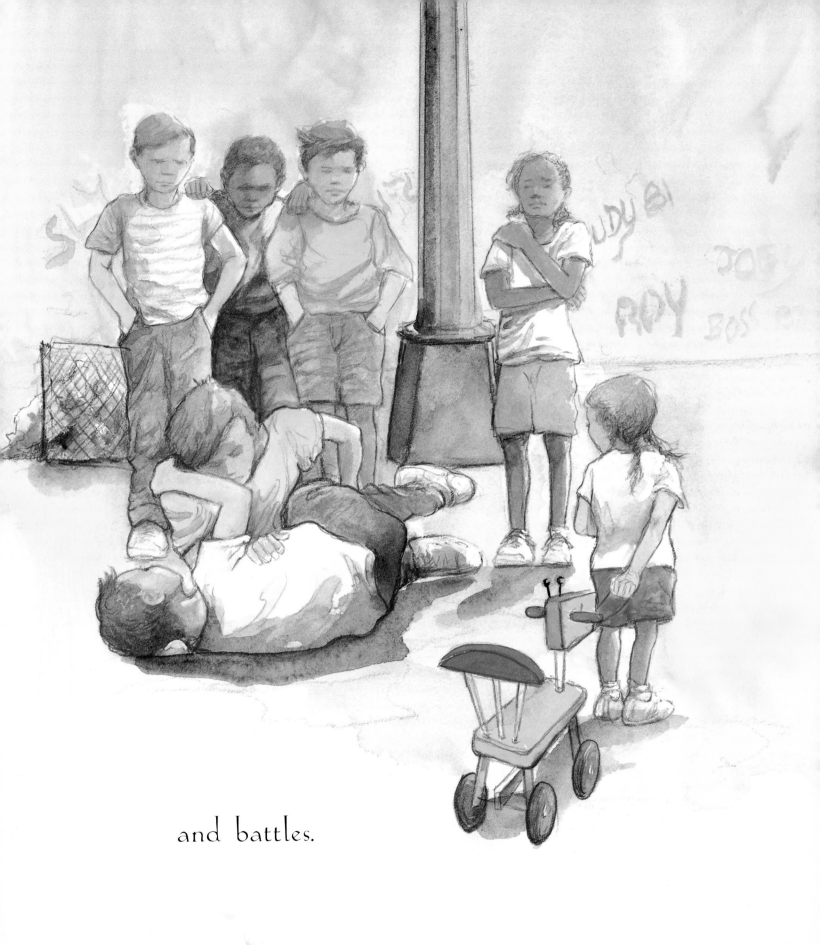

and battles.

She rode wild animals. . .

and flew with the birds.

She climbed a mountain and came to a river.

It was too wide to cross,
so she started for home.

The games were over, the fountain had stopped.

The magician had disappeared.

The wizard was sleeping.

But the magic box was still there.
It carried her gently up to her home in the castle.

From her window she could see the river,
too wide to cross on a yellow giraffe.